Indigo
the Magic Rainbow Pony

For Little Em, for always x – SK
To Maddox bach – ST

SIMON AND SCHUSTER
First published in Great Britain in 2012 by Simon and Schuster UK Ltd
1st Floor, 222 Gray's Inn Road, London WC1X 8HB
A CBS Company
Text copyright © 2012 Sarah KilBride
Illustrations copyright © 2012 Sophie Tilley
Concept © 2009 Simon and Schuster UK
The right of Sarah KilBride and Sophie Tilley to be identified
as the author and illustrator of this work has been asserted by them
in accordance with the Copyright, Designs and Patents Act, 1988
All rights reserved, including the right of reproduction in whole or in part in any form
A CIP catalogue record for this book is available from the British Library upon request
ISBN: 978 0 85707 224 5
Printed in China
3 5 7 9 10 8 6 4 2

Princess Evie's Ponies

Indigo the Magic Rainbow Pony

Sarah KilBride

Illustrated by Sophie Tilley

SIMON AND SCHUSTER

London   New York   Sydney   Toronto   New Delhi

It was raining at Starlight Stables. Princess Evie decided to clean her ponies' saddles. It was dreary work but, just as she finished polishing the last saddle, the sun began to shine. "I think it's time for an adventure," said Evie, happily.

You see, Princess Evie's ponies were
magic ponies. Whenever Evie rode them,
she was whisked away on a magical
adventure in a faraway land.

"Come on, Indigo," smiled Evie as she led her
beautiful pony out into the yard. Evie pulled on her rucksack
of useful things and jumped up onto Indigo's back.

Sparkles skipped excitedly around the puddles.
He loved going on adventures!

They trotted towards the
tunnel of trees. Evie closed her eyes.
Where would the tunnel take them today?

She opened her eyes to a kaleidoscope of colours!
Shimmering butterflies danced around her and all of Evie's
clothes had changed to rainbow colours – even her socks!

Indigo's mane and tail reflected the butterflies' beautiful colours.

In the sky above, a perfect rainbow glimmered. "I think the butterflies

want us to follow them!" said Evie. "How exciting!"

The butterflies led them to the end of the rainbow but, when Evie stepped out of the clouds into a garden full of grey flowers, she couldn't hide her disappointment. "Where have all the colours gone?" she sighed.

Just then, Sparkles gave a miaow and padded towards a wishing well. On it there was a map with a special rhyme.

The Sparkling Waterfall

The Mountaintop

Search and find each rainbow girl,
Collect their seven stones and swirl,
Swirl them in this magic well
Then watch their colours cast a spell.

Rosa's Summerhouse

The Sunflower Field

"I think we have to go to Rosa's summerhouse first," said Evie,
and off they went!

Soon they found Rosa. She was holding a ruby wrapped
in a scarlet handkerchief. "Let's swap!" smiled Evie
and she delved into her rucksack.

Evie handed Rosa a crimson ribbon. "This is for you!"
"Thank you, Evie," smiled Rosa, tying up her wavy hair.

A sparkling waterfall was the next stop on the map. Azure and Fern were paddling in the cool water. Evie found some paper in her rucksack and helped the girls to make boats that gently floated around the pool.

"Thanks, Evie," they giggled, giving her a sapphire and an emerald stone.

"Only four more stones to go, Sparkles!" smiled Evie.

Next the map led them to the mountaintop,

where Magenta was singing along with the birds.

Evie couldn't help but join in with the pretty melody.

"This is for you!" Magenta smiled.

She gave Evie a crystal stone in return for two

beautiful feathers that she put in her hair.

Next on the map was the sunflower field. There Evie found Saffron and Amber having a picnic. "I have something for you," said Evie.

She pulled out an apricot for Amber and a peach for Saffron. "Our favourites!" said the girls and they carefully put their sparkling stones into Evie's rucksack.

"Just one stone left," said Evie as they followed
the map all the way back to the garden.
But where was it?

"Without it, the magic won't happen," she sighed.
Just then, Indigo trotted off.
"Where are you going?" called Evie.

After a few moments, Indigo reappeared from
the rosebushes with someone on her back
– someone holding the last stone!

"I'm Violet," the girl said but, as she handed the amethyst stone to Evie, it slipped and rolled along the path. Even Sparkles couldn't stop it from falling into a deep, dark hole.

"We'll never be able to get it," said Violet.

"Miaow!" said Sparkles, tapping at the pocket of Evie's rucksack.

Evie pulled out a long piece of string.

"This will do the trick," she said, "but we'll need the butterflies' help."
The butterflies carried one end of the string to the bottom of
the hole and tied it around the stone.

Evie gently pulled the amethyst up.
"Hooray!" cheered Violet. "Let the magic begin!"

As Evie dropped each of the stones into the well,
the rainbow girls appeared. The water began to swirl
and a fountain of rainbow bubbles filled the garden.
Everything returned to colour!

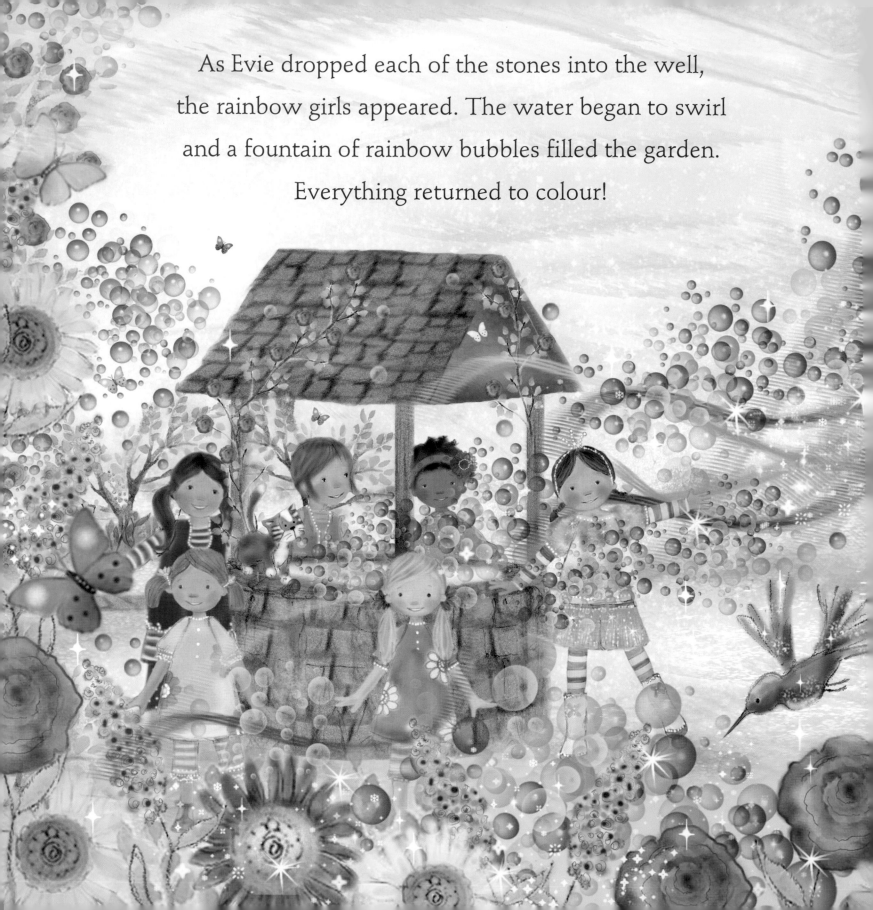

Shimmering butterflies and pretty hummingbirds
swooped gleefully through the rainbows.
"Hooray!" said Violet. "Let's play hide-and-seek!"

They were having such fun that, at first, they didn't notice dark clouds appear. "I think it's going to rain," said Princess Evie. "It always does," smiled Violet. "After all, you can't have rainbows without rain. You had better go before you get soaked."

Violet stroked Indigo's velvet nose.
"Bring them back to the rainbow garden soon!" she whispered.

Evie and Sparkles waved goodbye and
Indigo trotted back through the tunnel of trees.

Back at Starlight Stables, Evie took off her
rucksack and noticed a little umbrella tucked inside.
It was decorated with colourful butterflies.

Suddenly, there was a crack of thunder
and a rainstorm began.

Evie put up her new umbrella. "The sunshine will be back soon
and then we'll have a beautiful rainbow!" she said.

"Thank you, Violet and thank you, Indigo,
my magic rainbow pony."
"Miaow!" said Sparkles.

Also available:

Neptune the Magic Sea Pony

Silver the Magic Snow Pony

Willow the Magic Forest Pony

Star the Magic Desert Pony

Shimmer the Magic Ice Pony

Coming soon:

Confetti the Magic
Wedding Pony